Bella is a Bad Dog

BY MICHÈLE

Pioneer Valley Educational Press, Inc.

Rosie ran to the crate
and looked in at Bella.
"Why are you
in the crate, Bella?"
asked Rosie.

Bella looked very sad.
"I was a bad dog," she said.

"Oh, no," said Rosie.
"What did you do?"

"First, I chased Dad's car," said Bella.

"Oh, no! Is that why you're in the crate?" Rosie asked.

"No," said Bella.
"Next, I ate Dad's pizza."

"Oh, no!" said Rosie.
"I bet Dad was **very** mad.
Is that why you're
in the crate?"

Bella shook her head.
"No," she said.
"Dad was mad, but that's
not why I'm in the crate."

"Oh!" said Rosie.
"What happened next?"

"Next I got a little dirty,"
said Bella.

"Uh, oh," said Rosie.

"And then I got on Mom's couch," said Bella.

"Uh, oh," said Rosie. "**Uh**, oh!"